Blood and Ice

To my wife, Marion

Blood and Ice

Neil Tonge

A & C Black • London

WORLD WAR II FLASHBACKS

The Right Moment • David Belbin
Final Victory • Herbie Brennan
Blitz Boys • Linda Newbery
Blood and Ice • Neil Tonge

First paperback edition 2001
First published 2000 in hardback by
A & C Black (Publishers) Ltd
35 Bedford Row, London WC1R 4JH

Text copyright © 2000 Neil Tonge

ISBN 0-7136-5426-0

A CIP catalogue record for this book is available
from the British Library.

Printed and bound in Great Britain by
Creative Print & Design (Wales), Ebbw Vale.

Contents

Author's Note

On August 20, 1941, German troops of Field Marshal Ritter von Leeb's Army Group North had just overrun Leningrad's outer defences. To the north, the Karelian Army of Hitler's Finnish ally was advancing down between Lake Ladoga and the sea. It seemed that only the citizens themselves could save the city – once Russia's capital and cradle of the Revolution.

Over the following weeks the German grip tightened and Hitler boasted that the city would 'fall like a leaf.' But just as it seemed the city was about to fall, the German advance halted. Hitler had a more chilling thought in his mind. A siege of Leningrad would save him the cost of feeding almost three million people during the winter on food he would need for his troops. At least a million would starve to death and save his men from a costly assault on the city.

On 9 September, Stalin sent his top general, Georgi Zhukov, to put the city on a war footing. Factories, bridges and buildings were mined, ready to be blown if the Germans penetrated the city. Streets were blocked with anti-tank obstacles and razor wire. By 7 October when Zhukov was recalled to defend Moscow, Leningrad was ready to fight to the end.

And the end seemed only days away. Food was reduced to one-sixth of the amount needed for a healthy diet. And then the dogs, cats and even rats began to disappear. When they had been eaten, some people turned to cannibalism and in the market pasties could be bought said to be of human meat.

Eventually all that remained was a 12-kilometre strip that ran across the frozen waters of Lake Ladoga. By January 1942 as many as 400 trucks were ferrying supplies into the city. Every so often, a driver blinded by flurries of snow, missed the road marked out for the purpose and slipped silently through thin ice to a freezing grave below.

People died where they fell. A mother taking her baby for burial stopped for a moment's rest, never to rise to her feet again. For those who went out in the daily search for food their families were never sure if they would return. When the spring thaw came, and the bodies were found, the fear of epidemics grew.

Yet the following summer the worst was over. The bomb-damaged Philharmonic Hall reopened with a performance of Shostakovitch's defiant Seventh Symphony and the Hermitage Art Gallery began to put some of its finest works on exhibition.

But it would still take another two years for the Germans to be driven back completely. The death toll was terrible. Some historians have estimated over one and half million Russians died during the siege but history remembers the city for its courageous defiance against overwhelming odds.

1 ◊ The Riot

Afterwards they said we were heroes. But at the time it didn't feel like that. Each day was a terrible struggle – against the bitter cold, against hunger, against simply giving up and lying down to die. And if you survived all that, then there were 300,000 German soldiers poised on the outskirts of my city, Leningrad, with murder in their hearts.

I am Vanya Shkelov and this is my story of those dark days of 1941 when I was only eleven years old.

The food warehouse was a rage of flames, illuminating the dark December day. Charred roof timbers crashed into the carcass of the building, sending showers of sparks dancing into the oily black smoke that hung over the city of Leningrad like a funeral plume. Black, ragged specks of people ran or limped towards the burning rubble of the building, scorching their hands in a desperate attempt to rescue a handful of food from the flames. Their red-rimmed eyes were filled with fear and panic at the dreadful choice they had to make: be blasted apart by German bombs raining down from above or lose a scrap of vegetable that would keep them from starvation. The choice was simple in the besieged city of Leningrad in the winter of 1943: a quick death or a slow death from starvation.

Vanya Shkelov was not going to miss out on his chance to share in the spoils. Darting between outstretched arms, he jumped over fallen bodies, tunnelled his way through legs until he reached the front of the crowd. Being a small boy for his eleven years sometimes had its advantages, though this was probably the only one.

And there was the prize. Crates of winter cabbages had been thrown from the burning building and had broken open. An enraged crowd was now fighting over the bruised and shredded leaves.

Vanya caught sight of two women and a man fighting furiously over the contents of one of the crates. Their eyes blazed with anger. Scarcely able to keep on their feet, they slithered and slid as the cabbages fell from their arms and tumbled over the icy ground.

"Thieving scum!" screamed the man at the

two women who were attempting to tug the remaining cabbages from his grasp.

"Officious swine!" the women shouted back. He must be one of the warehouse watchmen, thought Vanya. All the other men were in uniform fighting the Germans.

A volley of rifle-fire suddenly stunned the crowd into temporary silence. It lasted for only a moment before they roared, screamed and began scattering in all directions. At the far side of the square, a thin black line of Russian soldiers continued to pour rifle fire into the crowd. Swelling pools of crimson spread across the snow where the looters fell.

It seemed such a little thing to die for, a few leaves of cabbage, a frost-blackened potato. But order had to be kept at all costs. If discipline broke down, Leningrad would be at the mercy of the surrounding German armies, who would simply march in and slaughter the lot of them.

And of course this is exactly what Hitler had planned. His army had swept through northern Russia to the old capital, St Petersburg, now Leningrad. Russian armies had melted in their path; surrounded and destroyed or marched off in their tens of thousands to die in prison camps. Now, barely three months later, the

Germans had succeeded in surrounding the city and were within 16 kilometres of it. Leningrad was completely cut off and the noose was being steadily tightened.

In this moment of terrible danger, civilians had been marched from their homes to dig trenches, build anti-tank defences and to string razor-sharp wire across the streets to stop the advance. Bridges and buildings were mined, with orders to blow them up should the German army break through.

Then, just when it seemed that nothing would stop them, the German tanks halted and the soldiers began to dig in outside the city. Strangely enough, Leningrad had been saved by Hitler himself. Instead of destroying Leningrad, the German leader decided to switch his attention to the capture of Moscow, Russia's capital. Besides, he reasoned, if his soldiers captured the city, there would be three million more mouths to feed. It would be less trouble to allow the people of Leningrad to starve to death!

Vanya grabbed a few crushed leaves and scuttled off down an alleyway. He did not look back at the warehouse. The screams told him this was not a place to be caught in. He threaded his way through a number of small side streets. His legs were aching and his lungs seemed to be on fire with the sharp, frosty air.

When he felt he'd put a safe distance between himself and the soldiers, he stopped, drawing in great gasps of icy cold air. He sank down onto his haunches, desperately wanting to rest for a few minutes before he made his way home with the 'prize' he had won for his mother.

As he struggled to catch his breath a shadow loomed over him. "Well, what have we here? A little food basket, perhaps?"

Vanya looked up into a face that was blue-lipped and hollowed by hunger. The man was tall but bent like a black stick. His outstretched hands reached out like two claws for Vanya, drawn by a cabbage leaf that was just visible above the boy's collar.

Vanya had little time to think. He rolled quickly to his side as the two menacing arms clutched only empty air. Scrambling to his feet, he sped off down the alleyway as the man threw shouts and curses after him.

This time Vanya did not stop until he'd reached the safety of his own tenement block. Shell holes had long since punctured the apartment walls and the whole surface of the building was scorched black with explosions.

Vanya raced up the steps and burst into his mother's apartment, desperate to tell her of his success.

"Mamushka!" he called out but then stopped dead in his tracks. He was not prepared for what he saw. His mother was talking in hushed whispers to none other than Andrei Zhadanov, the Communist Party Secretary of Leningrad, second only in power to Stalin himself. Vanya felt his stomach had suddenly been torn out. Was he going to be arrested for being in the riot at the warehouse? They both turned towards him as he came into the room.

2 ✿ The Mission

"Vanya! Thank God you're safe!" Vanya's
mother rushed to hug him, but he backed away.
His mother was always fussing. She had
wanted to send him away when many of the
children were evacuated but he had refused. It
was perhaps just as well, for many had fallen
into the hands of the Germans and had not been
heard of again. She didn't seem to understand
that he was the man of the family now, with his
father away in the forest outside Leningrad,
leading a band of fighters. Besides, he did not
want her to find or damage the precious
cabbage leaves hidden beneath his jacket.

"Please mother. I'm fine... fine. I'm not a
baby." Vanya crossed his arms over his chest to
prevent her crushing his valuable prize.

"Very well, Vanya. But you can't blame me for
worrying about you . Hang your jacket up. We
have an important visitor who wants to talk to
you." With that, Vanya's mother shooed her son
out of the room.

As the door closed behind him, Vanya let out a long sigh of relief. Before his mother could follow him, he took off his jacket and stuffed the cabbage leaves into the top drawer of the clothes chest that stood in the hall and returned to the room.

The Party Secretary was staring out of the window, his mind, no doubt, turning on the thousands of questions he must answer as the man responsible for the defence of Leningrad. How could they bring food into the city now that it was surrounded? Who could man the barricades against the German hordes? Where would they find ammunition?

Vanya studied the big man, who looked even larger in his military uniform. Small beads of ice had melted on his moustache and his face now looked like the sleek, dripping pasty face of a walrus. Zhadanov turned to face him. "Comrade Vanya, come over here to the light. Let me look at you."

The Party Secretary took Vanya's chin in his thick, calloused fingers and turned the boy's face to the light. "Ah, still the face of a boy but the heart of a man!" Andrei Zhadanov placed a fatherly hand on the boy's shoulder and remarked to Vanya's mother, "How quickly our children must grow up and play their part in the defence of Mother Russia." He drew his face up closer to Vanya's. His stale tobacco breath made Vanya wince ever so slightly but he did not turn his head away. "Comrade Vanya, do you love your country?"

"Yes, comrade Secretary. I would do anything for the Motherland." Vanya's chest swelled as he imagined himself as a brave soldier, standing stiffly to attention, whilst medals were pinned to his uniform.

"I thought as much. You are truly the son of your father – a brave, brave man. And you, a brave, brave boy, taking risks to deliver orders to him." Zhadanov paused briefly, remembering the risks that Vanya's father took every day on hit-and-run raids against German patrols. He was one of their best men. He could have had an easier life, for members of the Communist party got extra rations, but he refused any favours for himself or his family. If caught, they were shown no mercy by the Germans, who often hanged their victims immediately, leaving the bodies dangling on the gallows for several days as a grim warning to the rest of the population.

"I would not normally ask a boy to do this, but we need someone the Germans won't suspect and who is well-known to the partisans. You have often crossed the German lines taking messages to our fighters. You know all the boltholes in the city and the paths through the forest. You are our best hope." Andrei Zhadanov stopped and studied Vanya's face.

Vanya's face was glowing. What an honour! What glory! Would he be leading a patrol of partisans to strike terror into the besieging German army? This must be a very special mission for comrade Zhadanov to speak to him personally. Vanya glanced briefly at his mother, whose head was bowed. Zhadanov caught the shadow of the glance.

"Don't worry about your mother. She will be well taken care of. And I have reminded her that you will have your father to protect you." Andrei Zhadanov smiled and patted the boy's shoulder.

Vanya thought his heart would burst. "What must I do? Tell me comrade Zhadanov. I'll do anything."

"Have you heard of the Nevsky Cross? It is one of our treasures but – more than that – there is a legend that should it fall into the hands of the enemy, Leningrad will be destroyed. Can you imagine Vanya, if the Germans got their hands on it? They would fight twice as hard and our people would feel doomed. We must, must take it away from all danger for the sake of the city. Everyone will think it is still in Leningrad, but we can't take the risk of it actually staying here any longer. You must keep your mission an absolute secret. You must not tell even your best friends. If our citizens knew the Cross was being taken away, they would feel betrayed and think the battle had been lost."

Vanya suddenly felt let down. A cross? A cross? How could anyone think that was so important? Fighting the enemy, like his father, now that was real soldier's work.

Zhadanov caught the look of disappointment that flew across Vanya's face. "Vanya, this could be one of the most important tasks in the war. The safety of Leningrad itself could rest in your hands. Take it to your father – you know where he is. Then you will both take it to Moscow and put it into the hands of our glorious leader, himself, Comrade Stalin."

"Yes sir. I understand," said Vanya. But he didn't. How could carrying a cross to the partisans be of any use?

Zhadanov suddenly snapped back into the

soldier giving orders. "You will leave in an hour when darkness has fallen. These winter nights are long and should give you cover for your mission. Your mother has food for you. All the arrangements have been made. You will be escorted to our front lines and then it's up to you. Make contact with your father and pass the Cross on to him. If you are successful, Leningrad...no, the whole of Russia will hail you as a hero."

Unclipping his briefcase, Zhadanov took what appeared to be a small bundle of rags bound with string from the back flap and handed it to Vanya. The boy tucked it between his shirt and trousers. His mother returned with a crust of dry bread and an old piece of cheese. She was desperately trying to hold back the tears but could not stop one heart-felt sob. Vanya ate greedily, not because he was hungry – everyone was – but because he was keen to be gone.

"Take care, my son." She hugged him. But Vanya felt uncomfortable with this show of affection in front of the Party Secretary of Leningrad and wanted to be on his way.

"Don't worry, Mother. I will be with Father soon."

Comrade Zhadanov opened the door where two Soviet soldiers had now appeared and were waiting to accompany him on the first stage of his dangerous mission. As the little party left, the door closed behind them, shutting out the dancing candlelight from within.

3 ✿ City of Ghosts

The city of Leningrad had been reduced to a city of shadows. Jagged, blackened buildings, blasted into weird and tilting shapes stretched into the distance where there had once been elegant boulevards, shops and apartments gleaming with mahogany panelling and brass fittings. Leningrad, once a proud city that boasted museums and art galleries was now a broken beggar; its life ebbing away.

The snows came early and on October 14th the temperature plummeted to below freezing, adding another torment to the already tortured citizens. The old were beginning to weaken. Some had died alone in their apartments and would not be discovered for months. At the cemeteries, bodies were piled at the entrance, some wrapped in no more than a blanket. Above all, supplies of food were desperately short. And as the pain of hunger tightened its grip, dogs and cats disappeared from the streets, then the rats. Some families even boiled the bark of trees and ate it, or scraped wallpaper paste from the walls for the little flour that it contained.

It was four o' clock in the afternoon and the city was already pitch dark. Vanya and the two soldiers did not speak. Every sense in their bodies was alert to movements and sounds around them. Fleeting shadows that disappeared in doorways. The cry of a baby from behind a broken window or the despairing sigh as the last breath left a human bundle of rags slumped at the corner of a street.

They were heading for the only gap in the ring that the Germans and their allies the Finns had placed around the city – the tiny port of Osinovets which lay on the shore of Lake Ladoga just over 22 kilometres north-east of the city outskirts. Food, ammunition and petrol were ferried to Osinovets from the eastern shore of the lake. When the lake froze over they built an 'Ice Road'. As the only means into the city it quickly became known as the 'Road of Life'.

The buildings began to thin out to a few isolated houses and their gardens. Snow, tinged blue in the evening gloom, swept up to the lower storey windows, whilst sullen winter clouds hung threateningly overhead. Vanya and his guardians came to a halt at a crossroads.

"Vanya. We must leave you here. You know the way well. You have done this many times. Head for Osinovets. Your father knows you are coming. But be careful. There are German patrols everywhere," whispered the older soldier between gasping, cloudy breaths.

Vanya made sure the Cross was still secure. As he nodded his head to the soldiers, the older man grabbed him in a bear-like hug. "Take care, little man." He could not help but think of his own two sons, one a prisoner, the other dead.

After Vanya had struggled a few hundred metres, he looked back but the two soldiers could not be seen. He looked briefly into the star-pricked sky and thought of all those worlds billions of miles away spinning through the universe. He had never felt so alone in his life.

Vanya tried to take his bearings, for danger might strike suddenly from the gloom. He looked around. He was standing in a dark entrance with his back propped against a worm-eaten door. His breath left smoky trails in the icy-laden air. The windows of this burnt-out building which were not boarded up had shattered panes blocked with wisps of straw, old hats, lumps of mattresses and brown paper.

Shadows emerged from the inky blackness. It was too late for Vanya to think of escape – his back was to the doorway and there was nowhere to run.

"What's this sooty creature hiding in the shadows?" The voice boomed out from one of the dark shapes nearing Vanya. A hand reached down and picked the boy up like a wriggling fish. Vanya squirmed and desperately tried to break free. It might just be possible to slip out of his over-large jacket and make a bolt for it.

"Keep still, you little tyke." A hard blow across the side of Vanya's head left his ear stinging with pain. He must make his move now. Vanya wriggled free of his jacket and darted out of the doorway and into the frosty gloom of a narrow alleyway.

They were close behind him. He could hear them panting and the crunch of their feet in the snow. Fear leapt into his heart and down to the pit of his stomach. It wasn't easy keeping his footing on the ice.

Then, for a brief moment, the moon was blotted out by cloud and he found himself running blind. As the clouds parted he saw with horror, that – no more than six metres in front of him – there was a brick wall too high to climb. He let out a terrified moan at the thought of the pursuing shadows catching up with him.

There was only one chance of escape. Set against the wall was a crumbling lean-to building which housed a cess-pit toilet. It was smelly and overflowing but Vanya noticed that the brickwork had crumbled away, leaving, he hoped, a gap that he might just squeeze through. He looked up at the wall. Along the top was a double row of iron spikes. Maybe he could just manage to jump that far and haul himself over the wall by means of the spikes. Which was it to be? Over the top or through the crumbling brickwork?

Vanya dived to the ground and scrambled through the jagged hole in the brickwork. A hand brushed against his ankle but Vanya gave a sharp back-kick so his pursuer was unable to get a firm hold and the hole was too narrow for him to follow. Safe.

But then as Vanya tried to catch his breath, a hand came from above and squeezed him tightly around the neck whilst a foul-smelling sack was pulled over his head.

"Well, well, what little rat is this I've caught in my bag?" A voice as hard as gravel whispered into the sack.

"Who's there?" The voices of the pursuers filtered through the hole in the wall.

"Best gets you away to a cage, my little rat," the captor grunted to Vanya.

Half lifted, half dragged, Vanya was taken on a short but painful journey as the voices of his pursuers faded into the night. He struggled for breath, choked by the stench and the thick weave of the sack. A door creaked open and was then shut, followed by the sound of a bolt being slammed into place. Vanya felt the rise of each stair as he was dragged up to the first floor. Another door was slammed shut and Vanya was dropped in a panting, breathless heap on the bare boards.

The sack was opened a few centimetres and Vanya was dazzled by the candle that his gaoler held near his face.

"Well, rat. Welcome to the Outlyers. Don't try anything or I'll cut you."

Vanya shrank back and in so doing was able to study his captor. His cheeks were drawn in, his nostrils were pinched and his dark stubbly beard gave him the appearance of the devil himself. His eyes were buried deep inside his skull and his hair hung in matted folds like greasy wool. His clothes were black and shiny and every fold was lined with grease. And then it slowly dawned on Vanya. This was 'Hollow Cheeks' – the very same man who had nearly caught him after the warehouse riot on the other side of the city. He was an 'outlyer' – belonging neither to the Russian nor the German side but a survivor who robbed or killed from both in order to stay alive. He could expect little mercy from this man.

"Well, if it isn't little Food Basket," drooled Hollow Cheeks, as if he were about to carve a slice of meat from a roast.

4 ✿ Prisoner

Vanya backed away from Hollow Cheeks, terrified.

"Keep still or I'll cut your throat," he rasped. The menace in his voice froze Vanya's blood.

Hollow Cheeks grasped Vanya by the shirt collar and hauled him to his feet. As he did so, Vanya's shirt was pulled out from the waistband of his trousers and the Nevsky Cross, wrapped in its rags, was dislodged from its hiding place. It clattered to the floor, one corner poking through its cover, the gold glinting in the candlelight.

Hollow Cheeks' eyes bulged in their sockets. "What's this? Where've you lifted this from, Food Basket?" Hollow Cheeks screwed Vanya's shirt collar so tight that he could barely reply even if he had wanted to. The delay probably saved his life for Hollow Cheeks came up with his own answer.

"I knew it! You helps yourself to what takes your fancy, just like the rest of us. Stealing food or trinkets like this." Hollow Cheeks stroked the glittering Cross, caressing the jewels that burned red and blue in their gold setting.

Vanya was angry. How dare he think this of me! I am a patriot, not a rat in a sewer like this man. But he heard his father's voice somewhere deep inside his heart telling him to be quiet. 'If this man thinks you're just like him, you might... just might, survive.'

Vanya kept silent, letting Hollow Cheeks run on. A cackling roar of laughter burst from his black hole of a mouth, a mouth littered with slanting, stained and broken teeth. He slapped Vanya on his back, sending a little cloud of dust motes toward the ceiling.

"You're one of us! An outlyer!" Vanya managed a weak smile, hoping this might convince Hollow Cheeks that he'd reached the right conclusion.

"I could use a little mouse like you. Getting into holes I can't. And I know just the place." Vanya nodded his head.

"I want my share!" Vanya's threat suddenly burst from his lungs.

"You gets what I give you," snarled Hollow Cheeks. "But first we gets some sleep."

Hollow Cheeks bound Vanya's hands

together and secured the trailing end of the rope around the leg of a rickety pot-bellied stove. Vanya could just manage to turn over, but little more. Hollow Cheeks threw a couple of pieces of sacking at Vanya and the boy attempted to wrap himself up as best he could.

Hollow Cheeks blew out the candle, propped himself up in a chair, and pulled a greasy counterpane over himself, clutching the Cross tightly. Within minutes, the room was full of Hollow Cheek's loud snores. Vanya pretended to be asleep but he was too afraid to close his eyes. Clouds scudded across the sky whilst the room was bathed in an eerie, silvery moonlight. He was desperately dejected. He'd lost his jacket and the Cross and now he was a helpless prisoner in the hands of a man who would not hesitate to kill him if he tried to run away.

How could he escape?

The minutes seemed to stretch to hours. Though he was frozen, Vanya kept deathly still, terrified that even his breathing might provoke Hollow Cheeks to murder.

Maybe Vanya slept, maybe he didn't, but after what seemed for ever, he heard a rustle as Hollow Cheeks quietly pulled back the counterpane and stepped on to the floor. A loose floorboard gave a low wheeze. 'O God, mother protect me.' As a good communist Vanya was not meant to believe in God but in moments of true danger, real feelings welled up inside him. Vanya screwed his eyes tightly shut in a silent prayer, thinking that if he could not see then he could also not be seen.

Hollow Cheeks loomed over him, and gave a low grunt, satisfied that his prisoner was asleep. Vanya peeped through his fingers and watched him move across the room where he crouched over the stove and gently prised a short floorboard loose. The board creaked as it was lifted and Hollow Cheeks glanced over his shoulder to make sure his prisoner had not wakened. Vanya lay like stone but out of the corner of his eye he saw Hollow Cheeks place the Cross beneath the floor and replace the wooden board.

Striding to the other side of the room Hollow Cheeks lit a candle, for although it was morning it was still dark. 'Perhaps six or seven o' clock', thought Vanya, but it was hard to tell. This far north there would only be a few hours of daylight before night descended once more.

5 ✿ The Raid

"C'mon mouse. You have to earn your keep. We've got business. You'd better wrap yourself in those sacks, seeing you've got no coat. And just to make sure you don't run away, I'm gonna put you on a lead."

After freeing Vanya's hands, Hollow Cheeks tied the length of rope around his ankle and led him off down the stairs and into the bitter cold of early morning.

The snow had drifted during the night to wrap everywhere in a thick white blanket. After a two-hour trudge through the outskirts of the city, they scrambled across the remains of a bridge over the River Neva. Two miles further on they reached the top of a hill overlooking a cluster of four low buildings surrounded by a perimeter fence. The wire sagged with heavy strings of ice. Two grey-uniformed sentries paced back and forth at the entrance of the compound, occasionally stopping to scan the horizon and to clap their hands together for warmth.

Vanya could hardly contain the hatred that burned inside him. This was the enemy – Germans! They had invaded his country.

"Germans!" Hollow Cheeks snarled. "But they is clever and they is clever because they got the food and we haven't. Now that don't seem too fair to me so we is gonna share it out a-bits. Well, share it between us two and anybody who's got something worth trading. And this is where you comes in, Food Basket, 'cos you're small as a snake and snakes can crawl under wire and into cellars."

Hollow Cheeks pulled out a sheet from his backpack, which he passed to Vanya to put over his sacking so that he blended with the snow. He pulled out a second sheet, which he used to camouflage himself. Crawling through the drifts of snow, they inched their way towards the wire and the back of the nearest building.

"Under you goes, now," whispered Hollow Cheeks. "Head for the first building. You'll see a little window down to the cellar. There's plenty of pickings. Pop them into this bag and bring them to me. And just in case you start getting any ideas, don't forget I got you on a lead."

Vanya stuffed the bag into his trouser pocket

as Hollow Cheeks raised the wire, allowing him just enough room to squirm through and wriggle his way to the cellar window three metres further on. The snow had been cleared around the sill. Vanya tried to cover his tether with snow as he went along, in case a sharp-eyed sentry noticed a dark line against the white.

Lifting the window carefully, Vanya slid down into the cellar. As his eyes adjusted to the gloom, after months of starvation he could not believe his eyes. Shelf upon shelf was stacked with cans – of butter, of jam, of fish, of meat, of food he'd forgotten the taste of, of food he thought no longer existed. His mouth watered at the thought of the tastes and his jaw ached to be filled with this glorious treasure. He quickly slipped four small flat tins of tuna into his trouser pockets.

Then an idea came to him. He remembered a fairy story about a boy captured by a wolf and tethered, just as he was, but the boy had escaped by a cunning plan. Undoing the rope around his ankle, he gently pulled another three metres of rope slack and left it loosely coiled on the floor, tying the end to one of the stacking shelves. If Hollow Cheeks pulled on the rope he would think Vanya was still attached to it. Vanya hoped this would give him long enough to find another escape route so he could make his way back to the villain's lair to recover the Cross before Hollow Cheeks realised he'd been tricked.

Now Vanya had to find another exit. There was only one – a narrow skylight in the roof. It was dangerous, for he'd be visible up there on the roof, but it was his only chance.

He began to climb the stacking shelves until he reached the ceiling. The small window was sealed tight with solid ice and it took several minutes before he was able to prise the catch free and prop the window open. He hauled himself through the narrow space and slid down the roof, gently falling on the snow banked high against the side of the wooden building.

Worming his way to the wire, he tunnelled underneath and worked his way over to a small clump of bushes. He skirted the hillside and returned to the track so he could hurry back to where he'd been imprisoned the night before.

* * * * *

"Where's that devil got to?" Hollow Cheeks was getting impatient as he lay behind a freezing snowdrift. The longer he remained there, the greater the danger that the German guards would discover his hiding place. The Germans did not listen to explanations or excuses – a bullet was the only justice he could expect and that would be a welcome death compared to some of the things that could happen to you at their hands.

Hollow Cheeks tugged at the rope. Nothing.

"Lazy devil! He'll be stuffing himself. I'll show him." This time he gave a mighty yank at the rope. All he heard was a muffled crash as the shelf to which the rope was attached toppled forward, hit a second shelf and sent that one crashing to the floor. Hollow Cheeks was not the only one who heard the noise. The guards were alerted at the gate and raised the alarm.

Hollow Cheeks should not have stood up at that moment. But he panicked – the only thought in his head was to get as far away from that dangerous, buzzing camp as fast as possible – so he leapt to his feet. He may or may not have heard the crack as the rifle was fired. But then his head began to swim into blackness and he fell headlong into the snow.

Vanya caught the sound of rifle fire in the still

air. He quickened his pace. It wouldn't take long for the Germans to realise the thief had not been alone.

6 ✿ Escape

In less than an hour, Vanya reached the twisted wreckage of the bridge they'd crossed that morning. Just as he was scrambling down the river bank a German motorcycle and sidecar appeared above the brow of the hill. A machine-gun mounted on the front of the bike opened fire as soon as Vanya was spotted. Spurts of machine-gun bullets flashed from its muzzle, kicking up little clouds of snow in front of Vanya. He tried to dodge and weave but the snow was so thick that he fell over and rolled down the bank towards the frozen river.

The motorcycle edged forward to get a clean sweep of the riverbank. As it crept on, the bullets came closer to Vanya and he began to spin and tumble into its deadly path.

But the German soldiers, in their haste to shoot at Vanya, had gone too close to the edge of the riverbank. The overhang on which they were now resting was not solid earth but a drift of snow. The combined pressure of the vehicle and the noise and vibration of the chattering machine-gun split the overhang from the blanket of snow with a sudden loud and sickening crack, as if a bone had been snapped in two. Motorcycle and riders tilted forward for a moment, suspended against the clear blue sky, before they hit the bank beneath. There was nothing to stop their fall and all three began to cartwheel down the slope, sending sprays of snow and ice into the air like a glistening Catherine wheel.

Their screams could be heard above the roar of the snow as the momentum of their fall spun them towards the sheet of ice that varnished the surface of the river. They hit the ice at speed in a tangle of machine and bodies. For a while it appeared as if they'd come to rest on the ice but the surface was so slippery that they began to spin towards the centre of the river where the ice was thinnest. The ice cracked along a ten-metre length, the loosened sheet tipping forward to reveal the steely water beneath. The motorcycle slid towards the water first, increasing the angle of the incline. For a moment the Germans clawed at the ice-sheet to try and gain a handhold but none could be had and they slipped towards their death. Their screams pierced the winter air before they fell into the freezing grey waters and the ice sheet tilted back into place like a coffin lid.

Vanya was light enough to cross the frozen river without breaking the ice, but he knew he had no time to waste. Sure enough, two German infantrymen appeared like black crows on the skyline and began firing at him. Bullets whined into the ice or bit off small chips of masonry. But the distance between them was steadily increasingly and the debris of the bridge made it difficult for them to find their target.

Vanya scrambled up the far bank and made his way back to Hollow Cheeks' house. He waited while an old woman struggled to haul two pails of snow into her house and then darted up the stairs where he had been imprisoned the night before. He pulled the floorboard loose. The Cross was still there, wrapped in its shroud of rags.

Indeed, he felt a strange sensation when he handled the Cross. It wasn't merely the fact that it was made of precious gold and jewels. Now he sensed a power or presence in the Cross: a force that seemed to flow into him and make him stronger every time he touched it.

He'd been clumsy before. He must make the

Cross more secure. Taking a length of sacking, he split it down the middle and tied each piece above and below the arms of the Cross, and then strapped it around himself as a waistband. In a corner of the room he found a discarded jacket, which looked like a small coat on him. He turned the sleeves up, pulled on his gloves and re-wrapped the white sheets around his body for camouflage.

His mission had been interrupted. He had nearly failed. He must not make any more mistakes, for next time they could be fatal.

At the bottom of the stairs Vanya opened the door, looked left and right to make absolutely sure that no one was around, and quickly found the path which joined the metalled road to Osinovets and the Ice Road across Lagoda. It was midday, with the watery sun at its highest point in the sky. So much had happened. He must get to his father as quickly as possible. This time he would make no mistakes.

7 ✪ Capture

Vanya avoided the direct route to the tiny port of Osinovets, following instead the broad course of the River Neva until it reached the lake. From here, Vanya knew he would have to strike out north and make for the famous Ice Road, the road built on the ice of the frozen Lake Ladoga, the last link between the besieged city and the rest of Russia.

Two hours later, Vanya had covered about five kilometres north when he stopped at the edge of a short stretch of forest close to the river bank. The path directly ahead would be a perfect place for an ambush so he decided to circle to the east and enter the forest from the side rather than head-on. He followed a small gully to the right. During spring it would have emptied into the River Neva, but for now it was frozen solid and covered in a deep blanket of snow.

The stream bed was twisted like a serpent's body and gouged so deep that it was difficult to see more than about ten to fifteen metres ahead before a wall of scree and snow obscured the view. At least it provided a path to follow and its steep sides meant he could not be easily seen.

Vanya followed the path with difficulty. On the left bank of the stream the snow had been driven by the wind into high drifts. It was hard to keep his footing and he fell over several times, almost disappearing in deep mounds of snow. If only he was taller. Vanya thought of his father: he wasn't tall, but he had the courage of a giant.

With this thought still playing around in his head, Vanya turned the corner of a particularly sharp outcrop of rock. Suddenly, four mounds of snow rose from the ground. They struck out at him as Vanya stood in shock. He had walked straight into a German patrol operating behind Russian lines.

The German soldiers had obviously chosen the gully for the same reason as Vanya – to remain unseen. But they had been discovered, and the boy who had stumbled upon them must be killed.

The soldier nearest to Vanya grabbed him from behind. He clapped one hand over Vanya's mouth and, with his other, drew a savage-looking knife, which he pressed against the boy's throat. Vanya thought he'd used his head this time, but he'd walked straight into danger. The Cross had not protected him.

He closed his eyes, expecting the steel blade to rip out his throat at any moment.

8 ✿ Rescue

"Halt!" A second German soldier barked out the order, raising the flat of his palm as a signal to stop. Grudgingly, the first soldier lowered his knife. They then began to argue in hurried whispers between clouds of steamy breath. Although Vanya could speak no German he knew that they were deciding his fate. He had to admit, it made sense to kill anyone who might warn the Russians of this enemy patrol. On the other hand, they may want to be guided through enemy territory. Maps could only show hills, rivers and marshes; they did not indicate where artillery and army units were hidden.

It was clear that the soldier who had saved Vanya's life was in charge of the four-man patrol. He ordered Knife to guard Vanya and the two remaining soldiers to check that they were not being followed. One crawled to the top of the gully, whilst the other back-tracked along the stream bed. They returned within a minute and gave the all-clear.

"Sit down, Ivan!" the corporal said in Russian. He pushed Vanya down into the snow by pressing hard on his shoulder. 'Ivan' was the name Germans used for all Russians.

The corporal was tall, towering over Vanya. Several days of ginger stubble covered his chin and although he screwed up his face because of the blinding snow and to reinforce his threats, Vanya thought he saw a kindness buried somewhere deep in the wells of his eyes. He did not like to admit to this last thought. After all, this was the hated enemy. Inside, Vanya was a boiling mass of anger, blaming himself for being caught. He would willingly give his life just to pummel the man with his fists even though he knew he could be snapped like a twig. But, he decided, he must not give himself up to a hopeless fight. He must use his head not his puny, wasted muscles.

"What's your name?" demanded the corporal.

"Vanya." Vanya's mouth was so dry from fear he could barely speak, although he wanted to say his name with as much defiance as he could command.

"Well, listen Vanya. I have kept your life but if you are bad with us then I give you to Knife. Do you understand? He will have you as prisoner.

One wrong move and he'll ..." The corporal finished his sentence by making a ripping noise across his own throat.

Vanya nodded, his eyes wide with terror. He was trying to be brave in the face of the enemy but he knew these men would do exactly as they said.

"Do you know Osinovets? By the Lake Ladoga? The Ice Road? Your 'Road of Life'?"

"Yes," Vanya replied, but he had to swallow hard to continue. He desperately made up a story the Germans would be likely to believe. "My grandparents lived near Schlüsselburg and my mother sent me to find out how they are. I was heading back and thought I might be able to trap a winter hare in this gully." The words fell like a waterfall. Corporal clearly did not understand everything and held his hand up, telling him to repeat what he said slowly.

At last, Corporal said, "Good, good. Now you be a good Ivan and I do not give you to Knife." He patted Vanya's head as if he had been a good boy at school.

They travelled all day towards Lake Ladoga, keeping to the edge of forests, avoiding the charred remains of what had once been homes. The days were no more than a few hours long and so the darkness helped the patrol to make their way north without detection. Every so often the corporal checked his compass, making sure that Vanya was taking them in the right direction.

The patrol's confidence in Vanya grew. This was exactly what he wanted. Surprisingly, they had not searched him and he could feel the Cross pressing safely against his stomach as they trudged through the snow. There was little doubt that this patrol was a special commando unit, which had been sent especially to disrupt the flow of supplies along the Ice Road, the last lifeline into Leningrad. There were only two to three days of food and fuel left in the city. Staunch this flow and Leningrad would be starved into surrender.

Vanya clung to the hope of meeting his father's partisan band on the outskirts of Osinovets, from where they were to cross the Ice Road together and then on to Moscow. But any trap for the German soldiers would have to be carefully laid.

9 ✿ Partisans

The German patrol halted to the south of Osinovets where they hid themselves in a small wooded ravine that led down to the marshy shores of the lake. Vanya knew every centimetre of the ground for this was where he often met up with his father. What the Germans did not know was that about half-way along the ravine, perched beneath a craggy outcrop of rock, was a cave in which his father's partisan band had their headquarters. If Vanya could lead them to the path that ran just beneath the cave, the band could spring an ambush. If the Russians stumbled onto his father's band, however, it could be his father and his comrades that perished. He would have to find a way of alerting his father without arousing the suspicions of the Germans. In any event, Knife was keeping a keen eye on him, no doubt ready for any excuse to kill him.

Corporal gave the order to halt. They had arrived at a small clearing where several trees had fallen in the winter storms and which now provided a little shelter from the biting winds and prying eyes. Lighting a fire to cook a hot meal was out of the question and so they pulled hardtack biscuit and dried strips of meat from their backpacks.

Vanya expected nothing and so he was surprised when Corporal pulled back the hood of his camouflage suit and sat down beside him.

"Take!" he commanded, handing Vanya a strip of meat. Vanya was starving and although he wrestled with the idea of taking anything from a German, he decided it was best to appear co-operative. The meat was tough but welcome.

"Look! My boy." Corporal had unbuttoned the jacket of his uniform and produced a dog-eared and nicotine-stained photograph. "My boy, Wolfgang." Corporal's eyes lit up and his voice swelled with pride. A small, blond boy beamed from the faded photograph.

"Not seen for seven months." Corporal continued. Vanya studied the photograph. For a moment his thoughts were confused. The Germans were monsters. They had done terrible things and yet...yet here was a father who loved his son. How could they be loving and do terrible things? It was easier to think of them as monsters, Vanya decided, then you didn't have these difficult ideas battling away in your mind. After all, they were the invaders, they had started it.

Corporal's mind had flown hundreds of miles back to his home and his family. He was so absorbed in pleasanter memories that he didn't notice a shadow passing between two trees about twenty metres away. In fact, so quick was its passing, it could have been a trick of the dying light.

Corporal rose to his feet in order to put the meat and hardtack back in his knapsack when a single shot found its mark in the centre of his forehead, leaving a neat, round, red hole in the front but which removed the back of his head as it exited. Vanya stepped back as a fine spray of blood spotted his face.

Two of the remaining German soldiers took up firing positions behind the fallen tree trunks but Knife rolled across the ground at speed in Vanya's direction. Vanya knew that he would be killed instantly the moment Knife reached him unless he moved fast. The tree trunks had fallen in such a way as to make a V-shape, which narrowed to a dark recess at the furthest point from where Corporal and Vanya had been sitting. If he dived beneath them, Knife would be unable either to reach him or get a clear shot at him. If Knife stood up to attack Vanya on the other side of the logs he would be exposed to enemy fire. There were only seconds to think this through, but Vanya's simple desire to get as far away from Knife as possible plunged him into action.

Vanya moved seconds before Knife rolled to the spot where he had been. He felt Knife's hand brush against his boot and the panic made him scramble further beneath the logs.

"Swine!" screamed Knife as he sent a burst of automatic fire into the logs. Chips of pine flew in all directions as Knife tried to improve his angle of fire and Vanya tried to roll further from the deadly spray of bullets. A small opening at the end of the logs offered a shard of dark sky and the possibility of escape.

Vanya scrambled through the opening, nearly getting snagged on the broken branches. Once in the open, the deep snow made it difficult for him to run. He knew he was an easy target but the snow was so deep that he lost his balance, which, in fact, helped to save him. As he fell, the bullets whined harmlessly over his head. He pulled himself to his feet, sweating and crying with the desperation of his plight.

But Knife appeared to have forgotten all his training in his desire to snuff out the life of this traitorous boy. Knife rose from his position to get a better shot at Vanya but the action only made him a clear target for the attackers. Knife crumpled as a succession of bullets hit him. Vanya gained a vital few seconds to roll under a tree several metres in front of the logs, whilst the remaining two Germans were occupied defending the other two flanks of their position.

They would not surrender. There was no surrender in this war. It was kill or be killed and those were the only rules that both sides followed.

The duel lasted just a few minutes whilst the attackers maintained a steady concentration of fire on the German patrol. Both soldiers were wounded several times but they kept up their fire until, realising the hopelessness of their position, they turned their guns on themselves.

Vanya remained cowering beneath the canopy of branches until the shadows began to move cautiously from their hiding places and fill the narrow spaces between the trees.

"Come out! Slowly, very slowly!" commanded a Russian voice from the darkness.

Vanya wished he could disappear through the ground but they knew he was there. They'd shoot him if he ran.

Vanya crawled from his dark, needle-bedded lair back into the world of frightening shapes and sounds. He raised his hands high in the air, half expecting a bullet to wing its way out of the darkness.

10 ✿ The Ice Road

One shadow preceded the rest, a tommy gun cradled in its arms. Vanya stood absolutely still, not wishing to give any reason for the assailants to open fire. When the leading figure was no more than five metres from Vanya, moonlight pierced the veil of clouds and suddenly etched the human silhouette in silver. Vanya fixed his eyes on the square face that confronted him. Straight, wiry, steel-grey hair, a long thin blade of a nose flaring into wide nostrils and a proud, tight-lipped mouth that wore an unnerving smile.

"Vanya," he said in a whisper, "don't you recognise your own father?"

"Pappa! Pappa!" Vanya felt as though his heart were about to burst. After all he had endured: the narrow escapes from death, the fear of shadows looming out of the dark, and now...now he was safe. He could contain his feelings no longer and the words came out of him like a torrent of water from a breached dam as he was hugged into the warmth of his father.

The partisans had to post sentries to secure the perimeter of their camp, but then Vanya and his father Boris, still hugging one another, caught up with each other's news. Above all, Boris wanted to know how his wife, Natasha, was managing to survive the blockade. He told Vanya that he hated leaving her to fend for herself, but they were all under orders now. Life could only return to normal if everyone did their duty and threw the German invaders out.

"Pappa," said Vanya, ashamed, his head bowed, "I have been afraid. I'm a coward."

Boris gave Vanya's shoulder a hard squeeze. "I have a confession to make as well, Vanya. I am afraid too. Only a fool who doesn't value life is not afraid. Bravery is knowing your fear and still doing what you think is right. Besides," he continued, "we saw you as soon as you entered the ravine. You did well to lead them here. You are brave."

The partisan band made their way up the winding track to the rocky ledge where branches of cut pine disguised the entrance to their cave. Tomorrow, they would cross Lake Ladoga on the Ice Road and then go on to Moscow. Vanya curled up, close to his father and the warm embers of their camp fire. Despite his fatigue, he wanted to hang on to this moment and so he watched the flickering shadows of the firelight dance across the walls and roof of the cave. At last, when tiredness overcame him, he closed his eyes as a smile slowly spread across his face and he fell into a deep and contented sleep.

And so he remained until awakened by the amber morning light creeping into the cave. His father and his comrades were already awake and packing their backpacks. Vanya lay still, allowing the reassuring murmuring sounds and bustle to wash over him, until his father, bending over him, told him to make ready for the march to Osinovets.

* * * * *

Osinovets was a war-hammered port. Crumpled skeletons of buses and army vehicles lined the narrow road roads to the town, pointing to the graveyard ahead. This life-line had not gone unnoticed by the German Luftwaffe, who constantly pounded the town and its escape road, whenever good weather conditions permitted.

Lake Ladoga had been frozen for several months and its icy grasp had sealed the boats tight in the harbour. Those that had escaped from Leningrad now set off across the lake in trucks rather than boats. Some of the refugees had been given permission to travel, others had bribed their way out, risking the penalty of a firing squad if they were discovered. The price could be as little as a packet of cigarettes or a bottle of vodka, but it was a price worth paying for the chance to live.

It had taken nearly three-quarters of the day for the partisan band to reach the port of Osinovets. The town had just been attacked and thick, dark smoke curled over the harbour walls.

Everyone crossed the ice at night so as to escape air attacks. Every hundred metres, military traffic officers were posted to keep the flow of vehicles moving. Even barracks and shelters had been built out of ice blocks along the route to protect the personnel from the cutting winds that scythed across the frozen lake.

* * * * *

"Papers! Papers!" A sergeant strode towards them, his hand clutching the rifle strap over his shoulder. A torch blinked into life.

"Over here!" ordered the sergeant. As he read through the creased sheaf of papers, they could see his face visibly change, from scorn to respect. He stood to attention.

"You have been expected since last night. I am at your command, comrade."

"Then get us aboard a truck – and quick," snapped back Vanya's father.

The sergeant turned on his heels and scurried over to a circle of white-canvas covered trucks. His bullying voice soon got one truck driver to start his engine, which after an unpromising whirring start, spluttered into life. The partisan band scrambled aboard and after several more minutes they were joined by a convoy of thirty trucks that was to cross the ice that night.

The convoy was strung out like a glittering necklace as slivers of light from the headlights cut into the dark. The other trucks were bulging with civilians, some of whom had spent two days on the journey from Leningrad with only the food they could carry in their pockets. But the thought of escaping the city of death kept their hopes alive.

But then the lead truck coughed to a halt and the driver, leaving his cab, waved the remaining vehicles on. As Vanya's truck passed it, he caught sight of the ghostly faces of the occupants, staring wide-eyed and hopeless.

Perhaps they could draw off some of the petrol and make a fire before they froze to death. Most were certainly too weak to attempt the journey back to Osinovets on foot, even though it was less than ten kilometres distant. With temperatures well below freezing, the temptation was to lie down and be overtaken by a merciful sleep – a sleep from which they did not wake. Or should they survive this ordeal then the frost would make their fingers and toes so black with frostbite that blood poisoning set in if they were not amputated. But there was nothing anyone could do for the unfortunate travellers – the remaining lorries were packed tightly with passengers.

It was early morning before Vanya and the partisans reached Lednovo on the opposite shore of the lake. It was chaos. No one knew where to go. Crowds milled around in a frightened whirlpool. Had they come this far only to be abandoned?

But Boris's iron will had been forged in the long struggle against the German army and he was not one to be deterred by a breakdown in organisation. Clutching his son's hand tightly, he pushed his way through the crowd, his comrades following in his wake.

They made their way to the south of the town where Boris knew the train track began. Waving his documents underneath the noses of officials, he quickly cleared a path and he and his men were soon clambering onto the snorting train. Once aboard, they slumped down onto wooden-slatted seats. Streams of refugees followed them and soon the whole carriage was crammed with steaming, sobbing people, many of them on the point of collapse.

The train moved slowly through the night, stopping occasionally. At each stop an official came along, knocking on the door with a hammer and shouted out, "Have you any dead? Throw them out here!"

But at least there was food at some of the station stops – soup and cereal. Vanya and his father ate greedily, but some of the evacuees began to wretch and clutch at their stomachs. They had had so little to eat over the months that even this meagre amount of food sent their stomachs into spasms of agony. A few even died from the shock. The stench was overpowering. Stale smells from people unable to change their clothing and from the buckets that served as toilets, which frequently spilled over the top from constant use, made Vanya gasp for breath.

It was under such conditions that the journey to Moscow took several days. During this time, it was hard for Vanya to separate out nightmares from the horrors of waking hours. Here and there the line had been bombed by the Germans and squads of workers toiled to repair the track, whilst some of the dead passengers were laid out by the embankments.

But then they were there! Vanya gazed wide-eyed at the onion-topped domes of the Kremlin and cathedrals of Moscow as he and his father were driven by car from the railway station. Soldiers were everywhere, marching in columns, directing military traffic or posted as sentries on almost every building.

At last they had made it to their destination and they were on their way to see no less a person than Josef Stalin himself, or 'Uncle Joe' as the people were encouraged to think of their leader. Vanya clutched the Nevsky Cross on his lap, now safely locked away in a velvet-lined box, sent with the car by Stalin himself. What pride he would feel when he handed the treasure to Stalin – his mission complete!

11 ○ Full Circle

At last Vanya met Stalin – the great Stalin. At the time the man was like a god. His face was everywhere – on posters, on newsreels, in books at school. Vanya, like all the Russian people, had been taught to look up to him as the great leader, the father of the nation. Vanya's whole body tingled and his mouth went so dry he could barely speak.

As the great double doors to his office were opened by two aides, Stalin turned and looked in the direction of Boris and his son. He brushed the ends of his long drooping moustache from the corners of his mouth. Vanya had seen his image so many times that he expected a giant, a ten-foot statue, carved out of granite and yet, he could scarcely believe it – Stalin was small, just like Vanya's father. And his face, instead of the smooth skin in the posters, was pock-marked. It wasn't at all like the polished marble of his statues and busts.

"Welcome, welcome little comrade. You have served your country well." Stalin smiled and the corners of his eyes crinkled. He took Vanya's hand and pressed it into his whilst putting a fatherly arm around the boy's shoulder, squeezing it hard. As the bulbs from photographers' cameras flashed, Stalin said a strange thing – something which Vanya did not understand till many years later. By then he'd learned how Stalin had lied and cheated and sent millions of Russians to their deaths in prison camps, often for small crimes or even no crimes at all. Even Vanya's father disappeared in one of the camps, never to be seen by his family again. Stalin muttered, more to himself than to Vanya and well out of range of the others that were present. "Trinkets, trinkets. The people need these trinkets to believe in... to fight for."

Vanya became a hero of the Soviet Union, although no mention was made of his mission to save the Nevsky Cross. Instead he was praised as a young fighter, a true son of Mother Russia.

* * * * *

Now my story is almost complete, but not quite. Yes, the Nazis were beaten. The Germans were pushed all the way back to Berlin where their evil ideas perished in flames in 1945. Then the unthinkable happened. Stalin died, or was murdered, in 1953 and Communism itself came crashing down at the beginning of the 1990s. And the Nevsky Cross? That, of course, had to come home – to Leningrad – now St Petersburg again – the city that had withstood the assaults of the Germans for 900 days.

In the meantime, the part I had played in the rescue of the Cross during the war had been brought to light by a newspaper reporter. The City wanted to celebrate the return of the Cross and who better, the City Council decided than I, Vanya Shkelov – to do the honour of carrying the Cross to the Cathedral? Now, I wasn't sure whether I believed in God or not, but the Cross had played such an important part in my life that I accepted the invitation.

Surrounded by the shimmering blaze of gold cloth from the priests' vestments and the flickering candlelight, I held the Cross aloft with all the strength my old weak arms could manage. Then, lowering the Cross I placed it in the cup of the priest's hands, who blessed it and placed it above the altar. As I stared into its brilliant magnificence, I thought I saw, in the twinkling of its light, my father's face smiling at me. It was then, and only then, that I knew my mission was complete.

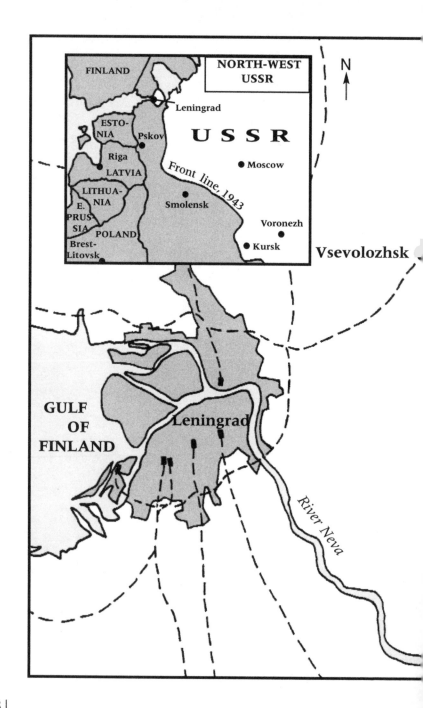

GULF
OF
FINLAND

Leningrad

River Neva

Vsevolozhsk

NORTH-WEST USSR

N

FINLAND

Leningrad

ESTO-
NIA

Pskov

Riga

LATVIA

LITHUA-
NIA

E.
PRUS-
SIA

POLAND

Brest-
Litovsk

U S S R

Moscow

Front line, 1943

Smolensk

Voronezh

Kursk

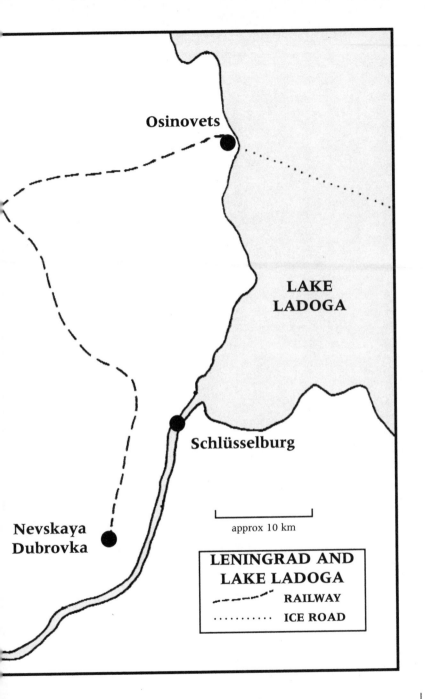

Osinovets

LAKE
LADOGA

Schlüsselburg

approx 10 km

Nevskaya
Dubrovka

LENINGRAD AND
LAKE LADOGA
– – – – – – RAILWAY
·········· ICE ROAD